Our Emotions and Behavior

Who Feels Scared?

Sue Graves

Illustrated by
Desideria Guicciardini

free spirit
PUBLISHING®

Last night, Kevin and Ravi
stayed at Jack's house.
They were very
excited!

In Jack's bedroom, they heard a noise.
Kevin thought it was a **lion.**
Ravi thought it was a **tiger.**
They were so scared they hid!

But Jack wasn't **scared at all.**

Jack said it wasn't a lion or a tiger.
He said it was Gus, the dog.
And Gus **wasn't scary**
at all!

Then they all heard a *really* scary noise.
It was coming from Jack's closet.
They thought it was a monster.

They thought it was a **huge** monster.
They got so scared, they yelled.

Jack's sister, Ellie, came in.
They told her about the
monster in the closet.
But Ellie wasn't scared.

She looked in the closet.

It wasn't a monster.

It was Jack's toy robot.

And that **wasn't scary at all.**

Ellie said she got scared
sometimes. She said
she was scared of
flying!

Kevin, Ravi, and Jack weren't scared of flying.

They thought flying **was fun.**

Ellie thought planes were **big and noisy.**

But she liked going on trips!

So she decided to play music
when she flew.

Then flying wasn't scary at all.

Ellie said Gus got scared sometimes, too. She said Gus was scared of **fireworks.**

But Kevin, Ravi, and Jack weren't scared of fireworks.

They thought fireworks **were** fun.

Gus didn't like fireworks that flashed and banged. He thought they were

noisy and scary.

So Jack always switched on the TV for Gus. And Ellie played ball with him. Then the fireworks . . .

. . . weren't scary **at all!**

Jack's dad came in.
He said it was time for bed.
He read everyone a story.

But it was a **very scary story.**
And **everyone** yelled and hid!

Then they remembered it was only a story! Jack's dad said that everyone gets scared sometimes!

Can you tell the story of Tom's first night away from home, staying at his grandma's?

How do you think Tom felt when he left his mom and dad? How did he feel when he went to bed?

A note about sharing this book

The **Our Emotions and Behavior** series has been developed to provide a starting point for further discussion about children's feelings and behavior, in relation both to themselves and to other people.

Who Feels Scared?
This story explores in a reassuring way some of the typical fears that children, adults, and even animals experience. It also points out that different things frighten different people and that not everyone is afraid of the same things.

The book aims to encourage children to have a developing awareness of their own needs, views, and feelings, and to be sensitive to the needs, views, and feelings of others.

Picture story
The picture story on pages 22 and 23 provides an opportunity for speaking and listening. Children are encouraged to tell the story illustrated in the panels: Tom is nervous about his first night staying away from home at his grandma's house. Soon he enjoys joining in a game with his grandma. Maybe he is reassured by his teddy bear. By the end of the story, he is happily saying good-night.

How to use the book
The book is designed for adults to share with either an individual child or a group of children, and as a starting point for discussion.

The book also provides visual support and repeated words and phrases to build confidence in children who are starting to read on their own.

Before reading the story
Choose a time to read when you and the children are relaxed and have time to share the story.

Spend time looking at the illustrations and talking about what the book may be about before reading it together.

After reading, talk about the book with the children

- What was it about? Have the children stayed overnight with friends? How did they feel? Did they feel afraid about sleeping in a strange room? What did they do to help them feel less scared? Did they, for example, find that a night-light made them feel better? Or did a favorite toy, such as a teddy bear, make them feel safer?

  Encourage the children to talk about their experiences.

- Extend this discussion by talking about other things that make the children feel afraid. Who do they tell if they feel afraid? Would they tell a friend or an adult they know and trust?

- Now talk about the things that might scare adults. Some, like Ellie, may be nervous about flying or scared of things such as spiders...or mice! Siblings in their families may have other fears, ranging from a fear of thunder and lightning to a fear of going to a new school.

  Point out that different things scare different people.

- Take the opportunity to talk about the things that frighten animals, especially loud noises such as those from fireworks.

  Talk about how to help animals at such times.

- Look at the end of the story again. All the characters were afraid of the scary story told by Jack's dad. Talk about the things that scare the children and how they can overcome their fears.

- Look at the picture story. Ask the children to talk about Tom's first night away from home at his grandma's. Can they see anything in the pictures that made Tom feel better when he was nervous?

What else can they think of that can help them feel more confident?

Suggest that children draw pictures of what makes them feel better when they are afraid.

Library of Congress Cataloging-in-Publication Data
Graves, Sue, 1950–
   Who feels scared? / written by Sue Graves ; illustrated by Desideria Guicciardini.
      p. cm. — (Our emotions and behavior)
   ISBN 978-1-57542-374-6
   1. Fear in children—Juvenile literature. I. Guicciardini, Desideria, ill. II. Title.
   BF723.F4G73 2011
   152.4'6—dc22   2011001626

Reading Level Grades 1–2; Interest Level Ages 4–8; Fountas & Pinnell Guided Reading Level H

10 9 8 7 6 5 4 3 2 1
Printed in China
S14100311

Free Spirit Publishing Inc.
217 Fifth Avenue North, Suite 200
Minneapolis, MN 55401-1299
(612) 338-2068
help4kids@freespirit.com
www.freespirit.com

First published in 2011 by Franklin Watts, a division of Hachette Children's Books · London, UK, and Sydney, Australia

Text © Franklin Watts 2011
Illustrations © Desideria Guicciardini 2011

The rights of Sue Graves to be identified as the author and Desideria Guicciardini as the illustrator of this Work have
been asserted in accordance with the Copyright, Designs and Patents Act, 1988.

Editors: Adrian Cole and Jackie Hamley
Designers: Jonathan Hair and Peter Scoulding